BREYER
Stablemates®

Penny

By Jane E. Gerver
Illustrated by Lisa Papp

Cartwheel
·B·O·O·K·S·®

SCHOLASTIC INC.
New York Toronto London Auckland Sydney
Mexico City New Delhi Hong Kong Buenos Aires

For Liz
– J. E. G.

For all children, who inherently know
good things come in small packages!
– L. P.

Library of Congress Cataloging-in-Publication data is available.

ISBN-13: 978-0-439-72239-1
ISBN-10: 0-439-72239-X

Copyright © 2006 by Reeves International, Inc.

All rights reserved. Published by Scholastic Inc.
BREYER, STABLEMATES, and BREYER logos are trademarks and/or
registered trademarks of Reeves International, Inc.
SCHOLASTIC, CARTWHEEL BOOKS, and associated logos
are trademarks and/or registered trademarks of Scholastic Inc.
Lexile is a registered trademark of MetaMetrics, Inc.

10 9 8 7 6 5 4 3   10 11 12 13/0

Printed in the U.S.A.   40
This edition first printing, May 2009

Table of Contents

The Test

It was the day of Princess Isabella's coronation. She would become the queen that night!

Everyone in the kingdom was busy.

They were cleaning, cooking, and
planning a big parade.

But the princess was worried.
"What if I am not a good queen?"
Isabella asked her fairy godmother.

"If you pass the test, you will be," said
her fairy godmother. "Do not worry."

"What test?" asked Isabella.

Her fairy godmother handed her a scroll.

This is your quest:
Search trees, water, and sand.
Look for twelve jewels
Shiny and grand.

This is your test:
Be helpful, wise, and kind.
Then, as a true queen,
Your jeweled crown
you will find.

Isabella went to the royal stable.
Which horse should she pick? The biggest?
The fastest?

Then Isabella saw her beloved Shetland pony, Penny. Penny wasn't the fastest horse in the stable. And he wasn't the biggest. But he was the smartest of them all. And Isabella liked him the best!

The Enchanted Woods

Isabella saddled Penny and climbed onto his back. Penny trotted down the hill away from the castle and toward the forest.

He and Isabella went into the Enchanted
Woods. The woods were dark and cool.
Penny had to walk slowly.

They did not see the crown anywhere. Soon they were lost among the trees. Which way should they go?

Isabella looked all around. Penny looked all around, too. He was hungry. He started to eat some leaves on a tree.

Just then, Isabella saw a baby
bird on the ground.

"Oh, no!" Isabella said. "We have to
help him!"

Isabella and Penny looked up into the
tree and saw a nest. So Isabella got off of
her pony. She picked up the baby bird.

Then she climbed onto Penny's back and
stood up in her stirrups. Penny held very
still. Isabella put the baby bird back into the
nest. Then she noticed something shiny.

Three emeralds! She picked them out of
the nest. She jumped down to show them
to Penny. He whinnied. She put the emeralds
into Penny's saddlebags. Together they
rode out of the woods.

Shimmer River

The sun was warm. Soon it felt hot. Isabella was glad when they came to Shimmer River. Cold water rushed downstream. But there was no crown— and no bridge.

"We will have to ride across," the princess said.

The rocks were slippery. Penny was
having trouble walking across them.

"Wait," Isabella said to Penny. "I will
walk, too, and it will be easier for you."

Isabella jumped down from Penny's back.

Whoops! Splash! Isabella slipped and fell into the river! But Penny was there.

He put his head into the water and pulled Isabella out.

On the shore, Isabella hugged Penny.
"Thank you, my dear friend," she said.
Penny nuzzled her wet hair. Something
shiny fell out. It was a blue sapphire!

Penny nuzzled her hair again. Two more shiny sapphires dropped into her hands.

"Good work, Penny," Isabella said. "Now we only have to find six more jewels!"

Dusty Desert

The sun got hotter and hotter. Soon there was no shade at all.

"Look at all this sand!" the princess said. They had reached Dusty Desert.

Isabella and Penny were very thirsty. But there was no water to drink. Penny stopped at a cactus with red flowers. He whinnied loudly and stamped his hooves.

Isabella used her sword to open the cactus stem. Inside was water—and three shiny rubies! They were as red as the cactus flowers.

Isabella put the rubies in Penny's
saddlebags. She shared the water with
her pony.

"Good boy, Penny!" she said.

The Mountain

Penny and Isabella crossed the desert. They saw a large mountain ahead of them.

It was getting dark now. And it was very cold. Isabella saw a cave and rode up to it. She got off of Penny to look at it.

The cave was too small for Penny to enter.
Isabella was cold. She did not want to leave
Penny outside. But Penny didn't mind the
cold. He was fat and had a heavy coat. He
pushed Isabella into the cave with his nose.

Inside, Isabella looked around. She saw a shiny spot on one wall. When she touched it, three diamonds fell into her hands! Suddenly, she heard a loud pop outside. She stepped out of the cave.

Her fairy godmother stood near Penny,
holding a crown.

"May I please have the jewels, Isabella?"
asked her fairy godmother. Isabella gave
them to her fairy godmother, who placed
them in the crown.

"You passed the test, Isabella," said her fairy godmother. "You were wise when you picked Penny to join you on your quest. You were helpful when you put the baby bird back in its nest. And you were kind when you got down from Penny's back to cross the river. I know you will be a good queen. Now it's time to go home."

The fairy godmother waved her hands.
POOF! At once, they were back at the
castle.

That night was the coronation.

Everyone cheered for the brave new queen and her pony.

"Hooray for Queen Isabella!"
"Hooray for Penny!"

About the Pony

Facts about Shetlands:

1. Shetland ponies originally came from the Shetland Isles, off the coast of Scotland.

2. Of all the British pony breeds, Shetland ponies are the smallest, but they are very strong and sturdy.

3. The average Shetland pony is 10 hands or 40 inches tall. Horses are measured in "hands." A hand equals 4 inches.

4. Shetland ponies are very intelligent and can be used by children for riding and also for driving.

5. The American Shetland Pony Club was founded in 1890. The American Shetland pony is slightly larger and more refined than its British ancestors.

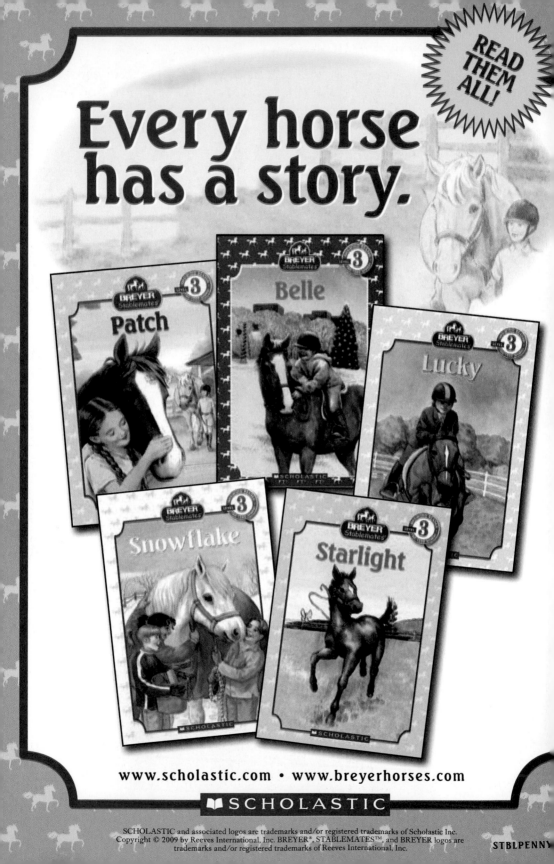

Every horse has a story.

READ THEM ALL!

Patch

Belle

Lucky

Snowflake

Starlight